The Runaway Chair

by

Pippa Goodhart

Illustrated by Polly Dunbar

You do not need to read this page – just get on with the book!

First published in 2006 in Great Britain by
Barrington Stoke Ltd
www.barringtonstoke.co.uk

Copyright @ 2006 Pippa Goodhart
Illustrations @ Polly Dunbar

The moral right of the author has been asserted in
accordance with the Copyright, Designs and
Patents Act 1988

ISBN-10: 1-842994-33-6
ISBN-13: 978-1-84299-433-7

Printed in Great Britain by Bell & Bain Ltd

MEET THE AUTHOR - PIPPA GOODHART

What is your favourite animal?
A cog (a cross between a cat and a dog)
What is your favourite boy's name?
Mouse
What is your favourite girl's name?
Annie-Mary-Susie (my daughters)
What is your favourite food?
**A fresh boiled egg with bread
and butter**
What is your favourite music?
**Brass band music to make me
weep and laugh**
What is your favourite hobby?
Keeping chickens (I got some for my birthday)

MEET THE ILLUSTRATOR - POLLY DUNBAR

What is your favourite animal?
A cat
What is your favourite boy's name?
Bertie
What is your favourite girl's name?
Sandy
What is your favourite food?
Chocolate
What is your favourite music?
The Beatles
What is your favourite hobby?
Drawing

For my good friend, Josephine Feeney

Contents

Chapter 1
The New Chair

"Don't sit there!" said Aman's mum.

"Why not?" asked Aman.

"This is my new chair," said his mother. "This is my best beautiful white leather expensive chair with class. It will go in the Best Room in place of that shoddy old chair that came with your grandfather from India."

"What's the point of a chair if we can't sit on it?"

"This chair is for our new life, Aman, for when we move to a nice area where people are rich and good." Aman's mother ran her finger along the smooth plump chair. It had a plastic cover over it to keep it clean. "I will invite my new neighbours and your Auntie Meena to sit in this chair. Then they'll see that I too have beautiful things that I care about, like they do. Now, go to school, Aman. Work hard and do well."

"I do work hard!" said Aman.

"You don't," said his mother. "Look at you!" She pointed at Aman's shirt. It was hanging out under his jumper. She pointed at his shoe laces. Aman hadn't done them up. "Scruffy on the outside and scruffy in the head!" Aman's mum said. "You know, Aman, your little cousin Bali can say all his times tables up to twelve, and he's only six years old. He'll do very well, maybe even become a doctor one day, Auntie Meena says. But you, Aman? You're a great big boy, but you can't even read or write properly yet."

She turned Aman round so that she could look hard at him. "When we move house we'll find a better school where you'll get tip top marks and become a clever man."

"I don't want a new school," said Aman. He tried to push his mum's hand away, but she held on tight and gave him a little shake.

"I want you to make me proud, Aman. Now, take your books and go. I have things to tie up and things to pack. You must get home early today because, don't forget, we are moving house and ... "

But Aman had already gone out and away.

"Alright, Aman?" said his dad as Aman walked down the garden path. Aman's dad had a spade in his hands and he was digging all around the walls of the house.

"What's the point of doing that when we're going to move?" asked Aman.

"It's what your mother wants," said his dad. He stopped digging to talk to Aman. He looked hot and tired. "She wants a better home."

"She wants better chairs. She wants a better son," said Aman. "Can't you stop her, Dad?"

"Not really," Dad said.

All day at school Aman felt grumpy. He looked out of the window and kicked things. All day at school he thought about everything his mum had said, and he got cross.

When Aman got really angry he decided to do something. He decided, "I'm going to run away from home."

Chapter 2
Leaving Home

Aman stopped at the shop on his way home from school. He bought biscuits and bananas. Then he didn't go home. He walked to the park. He went into the little wood. There was a grassy place in the middle of the wood where Aman could make a sort of den.

I'll live here, he thought. *That'll make Mum and Dad worry. Then they'll miss me. Dad will come looking for me. Maybe Mum will come too. It will be a test for them. Do they love me or are they happier without me?*

Aman put his bag and the food in his den. He thought, *I'll take what I need from home before Mum and Dad get back. Mum'll still be with Auntie Meena and Dad won't be home yet from his lorry driving. I need warm clothes. More food. There are some samosas left over from last night. I'll take them.*

Aman's mum made the crispest, tastiest samosas in the world.

I'll take my iPod. And something to drink. I left my mobile phone in my other trousers' pocket. I'll get that too. My toothbrush? Yes, but not the hairbrush. I'm not going to even try to be smart. I'm just going to be me from now on. Free me.

Aman ran home. He felt more free already because he wasn't carrying his bag full of school work. *I'll make a camp fire to keep me warm and cook things on*, he thought. *I'll need matches.*

Aman was thinking so hard about all the things he needed that when he ran around the corner into his street, he didn't see anything odd at first. He was almost at his front door when he saw ...

... that there was no front door. There was no wooden house with frilly curtains. There was just a huge empty hole.

Chapter 3
Moving House

"What?" Aman put a hand to his head. He felt as if all his insides had slid down into his legs, into his feet, and then trickled out through his toes.

"Where ...?" He felt dizzy. He stepped away, back onto the street and he looked left and right. Perhaps the house was playing hide and seek? Had it gone to hide behind another house?

All along the street Aman could see all the other houses in their normal places, all in a row, up, across and down, like teeth. But there was one big dark gap, and that was where Aman's home should have been. It looked as if a tooth had been pulled out.

"How ...?"

"Are you alright, Aman, love?" Mrs Jones from next door was looking over her fence. Aman looked over at her. Then he saw other neighbours out in the street. They were all looking at him.

"I'm fine," said Aman. He gave a little shrug and tried to look normal. But nothing was normal.

"They've only just gone," said Mrs Jones. "It took them all day to get the house onto the back of your dad's lorry. Then they drove off with it."

"I knew they were moving," Aman told Mrs Jones, "But I didn't know it was going to be today." He didn't say the other thing he hadn't known. He hadn't known that his mum and dad would really move the house. *Most people buy a new house and leave the old one behind, don't they?* Aman thought. *But you do sometimes see houses on the backs of lorries on the motorway.*

So now Mum and Dad had taken Aman's home, and all his things, and they had gone off without him.

"If you're all on your own," said Mrs Jones, "you'd better come in and have some tea with me. I expect your mum and dad'll be back soon to pick you up."

"No, thanks," said Aman. "I'm fine. Everything's fine." He looked over at all the other neighbours who had come out to look. "You can all go back in. I'm fine."

The neighbours slowly went back into their homes and Aman was left standing by the hole where his house had been. That's why Dad had been digging, he thought. Dad had been digging the house out of the ground so that they could move it.

Aman could see the shape of the house was still there, marked out on the ground. Aman walked around it. There were the ends of pipes, sticking out of the ground. Water and electricity and gas, he thought. It's like a heart transplant. First, you have to cut the things that keep the heart alive and working. Then you hurry it along to the new place and connect it all up again. Is that what Mum and Dad would be doing now? Finishing the transplant of Aman's home and connecting it to a new posh place to live?

Where had they gone? Aman didn't even know that for sure, so he couldn't follow them if he wanted to. Which he didn't. Aman felt a bit sick, a bit dizzy, and very empty.

"Where ...?" he said again.

"I'm here, you fool!" said a cross old voice from the hole in the ground where the house had been. Aman jumped back.

"Who said that?"

"Me, you young fool!"

And Aman saw the old chair that had come with his grandpa from India. It was lying on its side in the mud. It was the chair that Aman's mother had called Shoddy.

"Shut up, Shoddy," said Aman. "Chairs can't talk."

"And houses don't move?" said Shoddy. "And parents don't leave their children?"

"Shut up!" said Aman. "Leave me alone!"

Chapter 4
Shoddy

Shoddy chair was lying in the mud. It was upside down but its legs were kicking.

"Chairs just don't ever talk ..." Aman began to say.

But one of Shoddy's arms suddenly lifted up and pointed right at Aman. A hole in the back of the chair said very clearly, "Fool, stop telling me that I do not exist and pick me up!"

"OK, OK," said Aman. He took hold of one of the chair's arms and he pulled. The arm was made of worn old wood. It was smooth and hard. When Aman had been really little he liked to sit in Shoddy chair when he got upset. He would sit with his legs crossed and lean his head on one of Shoddy's arms. Then he would stroke and stroke Shoddy's arm until he felt better. The wood was brown and warm as skin.

"Are you really alive?" said Aman.

"Are you?" asked Shoddy.

"I think so," said Aman.

"Well, then, think that I'm alive too," said Shoddy.

As Aman put the chair the right way up, Shoddy crossed his arms. "We have to decide what to do about all this, you know."

"About being left behind?" said Aman. "I suppose we've just got to go and find Mum and Dad."

Shoddy's arms bent like jug handles, as if he had his hands on his hips. "Why?" he said.

"Why?"

"Yes, why. Why should we go and find them? Your mum and dad don't want us any more. They've dumped us." There were eye and eyebrow marks in the back of the chair, over a mouth hole. Now Shoddy's eyebrows went into a V shape.

"Your grandfather, your Baba, was proud of me, you know," said Shoddy. "He and I came all the way from India to Britain together. He would sit on me and think and talk and eat. When we first arrived here I was the only thing he knew in the whole country. He was a great man, your Baba. He never learnt to read or write but he made a family and worked to care for that family."

Shoddy gave a long sigh. "He was a great man and he was fond of me. But I wasn't good enough for his little girl, your mother."

"I'm not good enough for Mum either," said Aman. "I expect that's why they went without me."

"Like your Baba, you'll have to make your own fortune," said Shoddy. "Like him, you're now off on an adventure. Good luck to you!"

"Did Baba run away from home, then?" asked Aman.

"He ran all the way over the sea to a new country," Shoddy said. "So what do you think? Shall you and I run away now?"

Shoddy lifted a leg up and knocked the mud off it. Then he began to march towards the road. He turned and looked back at Aman. "Come on, boy! Are we running away or not?"

Aman felt a smile spread across his face. "OK."

After all, home had run away from him.

"Head that way," he told Shoddy. "We'll start our running away at the park."

Chapter 5
In the Park

The late afternoon sun was already hiding behind houses, making shadows long and thin. Most people were inside their homes, watching telly or eating tea. They had their lights on and Aman could see the people because they hadn't drawn their curtains yet. He could see them eating. He could see fires burning in their front rooms. Aman rubbed his hands together. He shivered.

"Cold, are you?" said Shoddy. "Then let's run!"

Shoddy could gallop so fast on his four thin legs that Aman found it hard to keep up.

"Turn left at the end of the road," panted Aman. Then he shouted "Stop!" There was a man on a bike coming down the road. Aman didn't want the man to see a chair running on its own. A chair – running? The man would tell everyone about them. They couldn't escape in secret that way.

Shoddy stopped. Aman lifted the chair up and carried it along until the man on the bike had gone past.

"Blimey, you're heavy!" whispered Aman, when he put Shoddy down again.

"I'm made of solid teak, you know," said Shoddy in a rather proud way. "It was because of my weight that I had to learn to walk. Otherwise your Baba would have had to leave me behind long before our travels were finished."

"I've never seen you walk before today," said Aman.

"Well, no. Why would I? I was a chair being a chair until disaster struck once more." Shoddy stuck an elbow into Aman's side. "You won't leave me now, will you, young Aman? If I'm found on my own I could end up on a tip. Or cut up. Or worse – put on a bonfire!"

"Don't worry," said Aman. "I want us to stay together."

As they went towards the park, the sun slid down behind the trees and the shadows suddenly all joined up so that everything was in dim darkness. "We'd better hurry," said Aman. "It's going to be too dark to see anything soon."

As they walked into the park, they heard the gates shut – clang! – behind them. Aman heard a high "yip yip" noise. There would be animals and birds in the park at night. "I'm glad you're with me," he told Shoddy.

Chapter 6
Free

"Do you mind if I sit on you?" Aman asked Shoddy. It felt like a silly question to ask a chair. He'd sat on Shoddy hundreds of times before. He'd sat and swung his legs and kicked at Shoddy. But that was before it got personal.

"Sit, by all means, dear boy," said Shoddy. He opened his arms wide to welcome Aman onto his lap. Aman sat. It felt nice after all the running.

"I wish we could have a fire to warm us up," said Aman. "Do you mind fires, Shoddy? Is burning twigs a bit like burning your family and friends?"

"Not at all," said Shoddy. "So long as the wood is dead and has fallen, then why would I mind?"

"I dunno," said Aman. "I just want to know what it's like being you. Anyway we can't have a fire tonight because I haven't got any matches."

We haven't got any of the things I was going to pick up from home, thought Aman. "They've stolen all my things, you know," he said out loud.

"Who have?" asked Shoddy.

"Mum and Dad. There are things in our house that other people have given me and that I've bought for myself. It's not right to go off with other people's things like that. It's stealing."

"Best to travel light if you want to travel far," said Shoddy.

"Oh, shut up!" said Aman. "If I was going to travel light, then I'd leave you behind!"

As Aman said that, he felt a hard prod in the back and one of Shoddy's arms pushed him right off the chair. Then Shoddy and Aman both crossed their arms and settled with their backs to each other. They sat in silence.

Aman pulled open his back pack and took out the packet of biscuits he'd bought at the shop. The sweet crumbling biscuit made him feel better so Aman ate another, and then another. The banana was sweet too. It filled Aman's insides and made him feel better.

"Not very good at this, are you?" said Shoddy.

"What d'you mean?" asked Aman.

"I mean you've scoffed the lot and left nothing to eat tomorrow."

"No, I haven't," said Aman. But he had. "Did you want some?" he asked.

"Don't be silly, child. Chairs don't eat."

"Oh."

"But chairs do like to know when they are going to be able to rest their legs on something dry. Are you going to find us a new home? Your Baba did, you know, when we came off the boat. He rented us just one little room to begin with. There was him and me, a bed and a small table. That was all. Your Baba worked hard and saved all his money. Then he rented all of a house, and then he bought a house and a shop. That house was much grander than the one little room, of course. But things were never the same between us. Your Baba found a wife and there were children. And all sorts of new furniture."

Shoddy gave a sigh. "It was never just him and me ever again. When he died I was moved to your place."

"I know," said Aman. "Uncle Ravi and Auntie Meena have the house and shop. I think Mum wanted to have them. That's why she doesn't like living in our street ... why she wanted to move to somewhere smart."

"Do you wish you lived like your Uncle Ravi?" asked Shoddy.

"No," said Aman. He thought of Uncle Ravi sitting at his desk. Uncle Ravi worked for hours with writing and numbers moving around on his computer screen. There were always worries about how well the shop was doing. "I just want to be free," said Aman.

"You're free now," said Shoddy. "How do you like it?"

"Great!" said Aman. "I don't think I'll go to school any more. And I haven't brushed my teeth or washed."

"Do you think that's wise?" asked Shoddy.

"Oh, shut up, Shoddy," said Aman. He spread his jacket in the damp grass and lay down on it. He pulled his back pack over and put it under his head to make a lumpy pillow. It smelt of the bananas.

"Do chairs sleep?" Aman asked.

"A good servant is never off duty," said Shoddy. He sat up with a very straight back.

Aman closed his eyes. He could hear police and ambulance sirens crying up and down the roads in town. He could hear an owl hooting, and something small was moving in the grass close by. Aman pulled himself into a tight huddle and shivered. Being free didn't feel the way he had thought it would.

Chapter 7
School Dinners

When Aman woke, he felt as chilly as a
carton of milk from the fridge. He could tell
it was still very early. The light was ghostly
grey. Aman opened his eyes and saw that the
grass in front of his face had drops of dew
on it. The dew looked like crystal beads. Each
blade of grass glinted with them. They shone
in the first glimmer of sunlight. Beautiful.
Birds were beginning to sing. They sounded
so loud because Aman was outside in the
open with them instead of shut inside his
bedroom. He felt properly free, outside, wild,

with the animals. But there was another noise that Aman could hear as well as the sharp bird sounds. It was a lower, slower sound and it whistled up and down. Aman suddenly felt cold and afraid. That spooky noise was only just behind him. Very slowly Aman rolled over and looked, but all he saw was the chair, slumped.

"Shoddy!" whispered Aman. "Are you snoring?"

Shoddy jerked and grunted awake. "What was that? Snoring? Me? Never!"

"You stay here," said Aman.

"Stay? What, here? On my own?" Shoddy sat up straight.

"I'll come back," said Aman. "As soon as I've got food and matches and things."

"How long will you be? Not that I mind, you understand. I just like to know these things."

"Not long, I promise."

The park felt empty, but Aman thought that at any moment something might jump out from behind every tree and bush. He felt very lonely. Shoddy is my only family now, he thought.

He thought of his mum, cooking and nagging and looking after him. He thought of Dad, always teasing him and smiling and working hard for him. *Are they missing me?* Aman asked himself. *When I'm all fixed up,* he thought, *I'll ring them up. But only when I can show them how I can look after myself. So the first thing I need is food.*

But how can you get food and all the other things you need when you don't have any money?

Aman thought about that as he squeezed through a gap in the hedge beside the shut park gates and walked towards the shops. Sometimes people begged for money and food. Aman had seen them, sitting on the pavements in town. Or they stole what they wanted. Aman knew children at school who took things from shops without paying. But begging was for losers. And stealing was worse because it hurt the person you stole from. Both of those things are against the law. You couldn't beg or steal and be properly free.

Aman made up his mind. "I'll earn things," he said to himself. But could someone his age earn money? Aman looked down at his shirt. He'd torn it, going through the hedge. Now it was the only shirt he had. What sort of a job could he get, looking so scruffy?

Most of the shops were still closed. A few people were on their way to work. Aman looked in the window of a newsagents. There was a notice saying "Room to rent. £150 per month." £150, thought Aman. And that's before you buy food and things! He stepped inside the shop.

"Yes?" said a man.

"Er," said Aman. "Do you need someone to do a paper round?"

"No."

"Do you want someone to … ?"

"No! I'm busy. Push off!" said the man.

Everyone seemed to be busy or in a hurry. No one wanted a boy to work for them. Aman asked the market people if they wanted help to set up their stalls. He asked a mum if she wanted help with her children. He asked a woman if she wanted help to hang out her washing. No one did.

Suddenly there were lots of children on the streets, and then there weren't. Aman stood outside the school and watched children inside, sitting in the warm classrooms with their friends. Aman frowned. Then he thought, *They'll be feeling stupid and bored, I'm so glad I'm not in there.*

Even so, all morning Aman stayed near his school. By mid-day he could smell the school dinners cooking. School dinner had never smelt so wonderful. *Mum's paid for my dinners*, thought Aman. *One of those dinners belongs to me.* Without waiting another second, Aman walked into school and lined up outside the dining hall.

"Where have you been?" someone asked him.

"What's happened to your shirt, Aman?" asked another boy.

Everyone had questions to ask, but Aman said nothing. He just looked at the food and thought about how much he could eat in one go.

Aman was sitting with a spoon full of apple crumble almost in his mouth, when he heard someone say, "Aman Singh, I want a word with you. My office. Now!"

Aman thought of how he would go into Mrs Henry's office and then the door would shut. He thought of how Mrs Henry would phone his parents. He thought of how his mum and dad would come to get him and all his friends would watch. Aman put the spoonful of pudding in his mouth and gobbled it up. He stood up. Then he ran.

"Aman, come back at once! Mr Parker, don't let him go!"

And suddenly Aman was running out of school with Mr Parker, who taught PE, chasing him.

Chapter 8
Running Away Again

Aman dodged and ducked and tried to hide as he ran. But every time he thought he'd lost Mr Parker, he'd look back and see the big man still there, shouting and running. I must get to the park, thought Aman. I must get to Shoddy.

Aman pushed through a gap in the hedge. At last he was well ahead. Mr Parker was too big to follow that way. He had to go round by the gate. Aman was gasping for breath. His legs felt weak. But on he ran, quickly into the cover of the trees. Now, he thought, Mr Parker won't find me here if I keep still and don't make a sound. Then Aman heard a noise that made him hurry on again.

"Shoddy?"

There was a large boy holding Shoddy while a smaller boy tried to pull one of Shoddy's legs off.

"Leave him alone!" shouted Aman. "That's my chair!"

The boys laughed. "It's not going to be a chair for long. We're making a fire, so shove off!"

Aman kicked one boy and Shoddy punched the other on the nose with one of his wooden arms.

"Run!" shouted Aman, and they both ran.

"What the ... ?" said the boys. "Did you see that?" And they ran after Aman and Shoddy.

When he came out from the trees, Aman headed for the park gates. There was Mr Parker. The look on his face would have made Aman laugh. But not today. Aman was running far too fast. As the chair and Aman ran past him Mr Parker took a step back. He saw the two boys following Aman, and he followed them. A dog woofed with excitement and joined in the chase. It began snapping around Shoddy's wooden legs.

"Got to go faster!" said Shoddy. "Run fast or you'll never be free!"

"Can't!" panted Aman. He thought his legs would melt away any moment. They felt weak and wobbly. But suddenly he felt something scoop him off the ground, just as his mum would scoop him into her arms when he was a baby. But it wasn't his mum who scooped him up this time. It was Shoddy.

"It'll be faster if you sit still and hold tight," said the chair. "Where to?"

"Home," said Aman, "Mum and Dad."

Chapter 9
Coming Home

People watched with open mouths as a chair with a boy sitting on it whizzed past. They froze still and stared. A few moments later they saw more people running. Some boys ran past, and a man, a dog, and a man with a camera and more and more other people who just wanted to see what was going on. But Aman didn't care about the people watching. Shoddy had his hard wooden arms hugged tight around Aman to hold him safe. He was going so fast that all Aman saw was a jogging blur of places and people.

"Left," panted Aman. Then, "Straight on." He thought he knew where Mum would have moved house to. It would be to the smart street where Auntie Meena and Uncle Ravi lived. It was a wide street with big houses and big front gardens with room for parking more than one car. It was a street where the cars were big, and they were often black or silver, and always shiny.

"Go round this bend, and our house should be there," said Aman.

It was.

Half-way down the smart street sat Aman's home. Dad's lorry was parked outside. Shoddy slowed down.

There was a lady next to the lorry. She was waving a finger in a way that made her gold bangles clank. She was shouting something. Dad was standing in front of the lorry. He had his hands up in the air as if someone was going to hit him.

"I will move it, I promise," said Dad. "But my son is missing. I can think of nothing until I have him safe home."

"Dad?" said Aman. "I'm here!" And he jumped off Shoddy.

"Aman?"

Dad ran to Aman. He left the lady still talking. Dad shouted to Aman's mum in the house. "Binda! Binda!" he shouted. "Our Aman is back!" Out came Mum. Her eyes were red from weeping, but now she had a big smile. She put her arms out to hug Aman.

"Hhm." Shoddy shuffled up beside them.

"Oh!" said Mum, her hands to her cheeks. "The old chair is back too! And who are all these people running behind you?"

"They're a load of bullies," said Aman as around the bend came the boys and Mr Parker, the dog, the man with the camera, and all the others. Aman's mum put her hands on her hips and looked hard at them all.

"And what do you all want? Eh? Eh?" she said crossly.

The crowd shuffled and turned round and went, all except the dog. The dog sniffed around Shoddy's legs, then it began to lift its leg.

"Not today, thank you!" said Shoddy. He gave the dog a kick and it limped off, up the street.

"Well!" said Dad. "So Grandpa's chair can talk and walk, can it? I think it had better come in with Aman and tell us what has been happening."

Shoddy and Aman told their story together as they went into the house. As Aman talked, he began to notice how small and scruffy his home looked next to the smart houses in this street. He saw a neighbour peep around a curtain and watch. He saw how her nose pointed upwards. Aman's mum saw too.

"They don't like us around here," said Aman's mum. "They think they're too good

for us, but they are so rude! Even when I make your father wear a tie, they say they don't like a lorry in the street. They won't even come in and sit on my new white chair! Even your Auntie Meena doesn't like us to be here," said Mum. "I think I shall have to get net curtains so that we can't see the look on people's faces as they go past."

"You can hide from the things that are outside you," said Shoddy. "But you cannot hide from sadness inside yourself."

"Goodness!" said Dad. "Where does a chair learn such things?"

"From listening to what is said by the people who sit upon it," said Shoddy. "I have had a good many bottoms on me over my many years. A new chair, however smart it is, doesn't know much about the world."

"Mum," said Aman. "I don't like it here."

"Neither do I," said his mum.

Chapter 10
Home at Last

Early the next morning, while the new neighbours read large newspapers and drank coffee, Aman and his family tugged and pushed and pulled their home back onto Dad's lorry.

"This feels like going on holiday!" said Aman, as they began to drive off. Then he frowned. "Where are we going?"

"Well," said his mum. "I suppose if we went to a really poor part of town then they might look at our home and think it was very fine indeed. They might think we were rich and important!"

"Do you want to be like the Queen?" asked Dad. "The only one at the top of the pile?"

"We'd be like the snobby people on Auntie Meena's road then. I don't want that," said Aman.

"Or," said Dad, "we could go and put our house in the middle of a field where there would be no neighbours, no one to see us and no one for us to see."

"That's not right either," said Aman.

"What shall we do then?" Aman's mum said with a howl. She was almost in tears.

"Easy," said Aman. "Let's go back home."

Aman's parents smiled at each other. His mum said, "See? Our son may not get tip top marks at school, but he's wiser than both of us put together. He's right. We should go home."

Back in their old place, the neighbours helped Aman and his mum and dad to unload the house from the lorry. Mrs Jones brought around a cake to welcome them back. Mr Jones told Dad that he had some plants to spare if he would like to make use of all that freshly dug soil. And Aman's friends came around to ask him out. "You can tell us where you've been and what you've been doing," they said.

Then Mum made some tea. She sat on Shoddy to drink it.

"I shall give that new chair to Auntie Meena," she told Shoddy. "It's just about big enough for Meena's backside. I'm proud to say I can still fit on you."

Shoddy settled himself around Mum's curves. "The truly rich are those who are happy with what they already have," he told her.

"Do you know, old chair, I think you're right!" said Aman's mum. "I have a fine husband and a clever son and I live in a place where they like me. I am rich! Richer even than my sister Meena. Maybe I'm richer than the Queen."

She looked out of the window at Aman who was playing with his friends outside. Aman was muddy and his shirt hung out and his laces weren't done up. But Aman's mum felt proud.

Barrington Stoke would like to thank all its readers for commenting on the manuscript before publication and in particular:

Kieron Amyes
Harry Bassett
Ryan Beer
Katy Burke
Shane Butts
Lee Chaffe
Thomas Clarke
Sophie Condlyffe
Sarah Dunn
Scott Fielding
Corieanne Foley
Olivia Fordyce

Carol Foreman
Charlotte Heath
Bethany Jones
Alex Kinder
Cari Miles
Karma Morgan
Rhodri Richards
Hannah Robinson
Charlotte Rowberry
Edward Sainsbury
Chris Symon
Susan Wheeler

Become a Consultant!

Would you like to give us feedback on our titles before they are published? Contact us at the email address below – we'd love to hear from you!

info@barringtonstoke.co.uk
www.barringtonstoke.co.uk

More exciting new titles ...

Enna Hittims
by
Diana Wynne Jones

Anne Smith is sick of being sick. So she makes up stories about Enna Hittims – a brave hero, as big as Anne's finger, with a magic sword that cuts anything. It's the best game ever ... until Enna comes to life!

You can order *Enna Hittims* directly from our website at: **www.barringtonstoke.co.uk**

More exciting new titles ...

King John and the Abbot

by

Jan Mark

King John – Rich but greedy. He has all of England.

The Abbot – Rich but rude. He has a problem.

The Shepherd – Poor, but clever. He has nothing at all (except a scruffy dog).

King John has given the Abbot 3 puzzles. If the Abbot gets them wrong, King john will cut off his head! Can Jack save the Abbot's neck?

You can order *King John and the Abbot* directly from our website at: **www.barringtonstoke.co.uk**